GREEN MAN ASCENDANT

Praise for A J Dalton's writing

Fantasy-Faction.com: 'Unique ideas and a story that develops in an unpredictable manner.'

SFX: 'Gives you an interesting setting and a devilishly good villain.'

SciFi Now: 'Engaging, filled with sacrifice, adventure and some very bloody battles!'

Waterstones central buyer: 'The best young British fantasy author on the circuit at the moment.'

Sfbook.com: 'Very, very clever and manages to offer something different over the traditional fantasy fare. Different, fresh and unique.'

FantasyBookReview.co.uk: 'With its rich tapestry of characters and incident there is never a dull moment.'

The Eloquent Page: 'There's interesting world-building to discover and a surprising amount of dry humour to enjoy. A great deal of fun and certainly worthy of your time!'

IWillReadBooks.com: 'A J Dalton's world-building is fresh with new ideas.'

Amazon.co.uk: 'Fast-moving and keeps you gripped at all times, while also creating a world with immense depth and complexity. Five stars!'

GoodReads.com: 'A J Dalton, thank you; what I've read will stay with me for a long time.'

GREEN MAN ASCENDANT

poems by
A J Dalton

Wild Man of the Woods Press

FIRST TRADE PAPERBACK EDITION

ISBN: 979-8-9930162-3-8

Editor and Publisher, Justin T. O'Conor Sloane
Cover art: *The Barley Tower* © 2025 by Bruce Pennington
Cover design by Katerina Bruno
Interior design & layout by F. J. Bergmann

Wild Man of the Woods Press
an imprint of Starship Sloane Publishing Company, Inc.
Austin–Round Rock, Texas
starshipsloane.com

*Dedicated to all
those who venture
into the dark woods*

Table of Contents

Foreword by Adam Dalton-West (A J Dalton)   xi

LOST GODS

Herne Ascendant,
    or the Final Season of the Green Man   3

Hunting Herne   5

Herne Fallen   6

Herne Rising   8

Stave Kirk Survivor   10

Jupiter   11

Grail   12

LOST MONSTERS

The Loch   17

Centre of the Labyrinth   19

Hydra   20

Wyvern   21

Cyclops   22

Roc   23

Mari Lywd   24

LOST TIMES

Song of the Crannóg   27

Ultima Thule   29

The Broch of Gurness   30

Vikingr   31

Golem 32

Banshee 34

LOST WORLDS

radon daughter 37

The Archaeology of Yarn 38

The Iridescent Seas of Yarn 39

The Ghosts of Yarn 40

An Intergalactic Interlude 42

Penal Colony 045 43

NEW REALITIES

Superstring 47

Chronovirus 48

A Public Safety Announcement 49

The Surgeon 51

The Simulation 52

Technorati 54

NEW REALMS

Gulliver's Travels to the Farthest Reaches 59

Spirit Sleuth 64

Cloud People 66

On a Wing and a Prayer 67

Darker Darkest 68

Nether Realm 69

NEW DARKNESSES

Denizens 73

The Ritual   74

The Dark Magician   75

Man Grove   77

Phantasm   78

Ecohorror II   79

New Dreams

The Starry Night   83

After Marianne Stokes   84

Technocracy   85

Technosavant   86

Technomancer   87

Designing Daisies   88

Acknowledgements   91

About the Author   93

Foreword

Speculative poetry typically involves works of science fiction, fantasy, horror and the weird. Since it is genre-related, it tends to have strong narrative arcs and characterization. As a literary tradition, though, it pre-dates contemporary definitions of genre, with epic poems about gods and monsters (like the *Iliad* and the *Odyssey*), fantastical poems like *Beowulf*, satirical poems involving encounters with the devil as in the *Canterbury Tales*, and poetry about magicians and elementals as in Shakespeare's *The Tempest*. Speculative poetry, then, is both an oral and literary tradition that is foundational to early cultures and societies. Indeed, such poetry was, more often than not, performed aloud within communities (since many in the audience were likely to have been non-literate), to share values, life lessons, ancestral history, the 'law', other knowledge and faith, all to build a shared identity. That might explain why such poetry is so frequent and essential to the fabric and world-building in Tolkien's *The Lord of the Rings*.

Happily, there is still a thriving demand for speculative poetry, with a slew of journals and magazines for international audiences. A leading title is *Star*Line* journal, published by the Science Fiction & Fantasy Poetry Association (SFPA), which also oversees the annual Rhysling Award. Other US titles include *Asimov's Science Fiction, Analog, Worlds of IF, Strange Horizons, Space & Time*, and many more. Meanwhile, the UK offers *BFS Horizons, Gothic Nature Journal, Shoreline of Infinity* and others. Canada brings us *On Spec Magazine, Augur Magazine* and *Polar Borealis*, to name but a few, and Australia gives us *Andromeda Spaceways Inflight Magazine* and a legacy of other worthy titles.

Speculative poetry is also naturally related to speculative fiction, which was defined in legendary US sci-fi writer Robert Heinlein's 1947 essay 'On the Writing of Speculative Fiction'. He identified the two key elements of speculative fiction as the part 'about people' and the part 'about gadgets'. Furthermore, it was

Heinlein who identified the underlying 'What would happen if—' dynamic and motif that, even today, instigates or underpins the speculative. For all that Heinlein's essay still carries a particular authority; however, he opens his essay by quoting Rudyard Kipling and referencing a poetic literary tradition rather than a short story or novelistic one:

> *There are nine-and-sixty ways*
> *Of constructing tribal lays*
> *And every single one of them is right*

It suggests Heinlein himself was wary of being overly prescriptive or definitive, perhaps understanding that to be so convergent was at odds with the divergent and evolving nature of the speculative, a tendency that implicitly undertakes explorative and creative research in order to (and only in order to) break new ground (and provide an original vision and contribution to knowledge). It also strongly suggests that Heinlein understood the nature of the speculative as extending to older traditions, other cultures, ideas and forms beyond the short story and novel-based concerns and interests of his own essay and Western constituency.

From the above, we can now understand something of why the nature of speculative poetry can never be entirely pinned down— the pinning itself would be to kill the butterfly, perhaps, a creature which is so much more beautiful when flying free. Any definition of speculative poetry is, by definition, too limited and limiting.

How then best to understand and appreciate the nature of speculative poetry? Why, by experiencing it, by reading it, more and more. Certainly Adam Dalton-West (aka AJ Dalton), the author of this collection, thrills in the new vistas and sense of place speculative poetry has brought him. He is happy to venture that speculative poetry (both the reading and writing involved) has changed him as a person, and he only wishes to share its potential with others. Many of the poems in this collection *Green Man Ascendant* have been individually published in the journals and magazines mentioned in this Foreword—but they are gathered together here for the first time. Indeed, the poem 'Chronovirus' was most recently published by the prestigious *Star*Line* journal. It captures something of the whimsical loneliness that, arguably, we all share.

Adam Dalton-West (writing as A J Dalton)
London, 4 April 2025
www.ajdalton.eu

LOST GODS

Herne Ascendant, or the Final Season of the Green Man

Desiccated earth puffed up in clouds
to mix with particulate pollution
refracts the light so prettily:
beautiful rainbows framing
the dusty waste stretching
as far as the watery eye
can hardly see.

It's fortunate the crops are failing
some might say: it controls the …
population, in a humane way
– the fewer, the better
or so I've heard
if we ever want to recover
assuming that's even possible.

The labs have stored, we're reassured
sufficient animal DNA
to resurrect all that was:
except with fewer humans, I guess
and I'm not sure who's kept
for bringing back, and who's
well, earmarked for the next life.

There'd been talk of a Mars colony –
whatever happened to that?
– it was our last best hope

wasn't it? or just the fancy of elite
dreamers brought up on stories
of Neverland, where we fight pirates
and play the entire eternal afternoon.

The stars are no longer visible
in the murk, though I like to think
they're there, like coins thrown
into a well with a wish
or lost in the mud waiting
to be found by future generations
or serious archaeologists.

Hunger is a healthy appetite
right? a relish of exquisite taste
to transform worms, wood
and even clothing into wondrous meals
keeping us going long enough
dizzily to imagine we spied
a shiny new blade of grass, there thrusting upwards.

Hunting Herne

When did you get so shy
since they labelled you toxic
levelled the land and cleared you out?
Are you one of the homeless
dossing under the flyover
addled in urine and off your head?
Do you ask for handouts
to swap for fentanyl and forgetting
or maybe you're on state benefits
declared unfit for work
your hounds all in the pound
and not so many great stags found
hereabouts among the car parks
wheely bins, collection points
back alleys and doorways all shooting up?
Maybe you sold your horns
to make ends meet
knowing to stand out from the herd
a sure way to become prey.
Are they mounted as a trophy
in a baronial feasting hall
where hen-dos and tourists
scream for entertainment, ale
motley jesters and male strippers?
Perhaps, though, just perhaps
there's still a vestige of deep forest
overlooked between HS1 and 2
where you reside and bide your time
waiting on a final pandemic and species collapse
when at last all chaos and wild abandon
will come to rule once more.

Herne Fallen

Old god
though you claimed to be
an arrest warrant was issued
for your hunting
without a licence.

I've seen your WANTED poster
horns and all
though none dares mention them
– even awkwardly –
as if a disability.

Poacher! Outlaw! Monster!
or so they call you
the lairds alone permitted
their sport, all else fugitive
and fair game.

It's no longer
allowed in Scotland, you see
meaning a cull of deer
is richly required
each year.

They forbid
even fishing
imagine
there –
but for the grace.

And so you were
imprisoned
a wild animal
too dangerous to be allowed
freedom.

Herne Rising

And you had gawking visitors:
too curious tourists
zoo-loopy groupies
wishy-washy well-wishers
jolly journos and, bizarrely
a cringing Christian chaplain.

And the abnormality of your antlers
saw them pity you
like nothing else:
a birth defect, an affliction
differently abled
a victim rather than in possession
of an offensive weapon.

Till a wild campaign arose
against your incarceration
public opinion outraged
they should do this
to you, an itinerant
homeless and marginalised.

Till they allowed you
– as shining symbol enshrined
of all society's evils –
to lead the Great Hunt
once more, of prey
hounds baying and coursing
as in days of yore.

And something was restored
perhaps, in the wild abandon
of chase and thrilled exhaustion
though you didn't choose
to linger long, wisely
retreating amongst the trees.

Stave Kirk Survivor

one by one
his churches burned
and the god retreated
till he hid among the rafters
of his final house
hidden
in the deep
near-forgotten valley

a single worshipper
remained
bent-backed, decrepit
mumbling of monsters
dream-demons and death
till the divinity seized him
cruelly straightened his spine
and sent him anew

into the world
a last prophet and promise
of what faith could bring
eternal life
an end to strife
sainted soldiers marching
to reclaim the minds
of the lost and found

Jupiter

Worship me, mortal
For it is my due
Court not my displeasure
Or my wrath will befall you
Your house will be toppled
Your children undone
Your crops will be withered
And your herds will then sicken.

Rightly fear me, mortal
And learn to know your place
Dare not challenge the gods
Or you'll damn your whole race
Your towns will be buried
By volcano, sea and quake
Your islands will drown
Your history erased.

Come celebrate me, mortal
In music, dance and ode
Build my statues and temples
My transport and roads
So armies can march
To spread the good word
My empire is come
And my will must be done.

Grail

we ran the deepest
searches and dug the predicted
places all to no avail
– so secured certain symbologists
to scrutinise the stars
mumble over musty maps
and interpret ancient arts
– they led us to mausolea
down dark and winding wells
to forgotten chambers beneath the ground:
only dusty bones were found

instead we went to historians
geographers and priests
who took us round the world
and back on a hunch
and wayward prayer
till at last an astrophysicist
pointed to the heavens
of course! we should have known
before we came from up on high
– our quest would see us rise once more
into the glorious skies

the mighty fleet assembled
to lead the great ascension
our telescopes were surely trained
on the likeliest of targets:
we criss-crossed the void
with crucifixes
like templar knights reborn

as if to storm Jerusalem
through which we might be saved
the prize would surely now be ours
yet all there was … was nothing

LOST MONSTERS

The Loch

It seems
the old stories were right
why didn't we listen
just because
a ripple wasn't seen
on the surface
in years?

Still waters
run deep, all know that
yet we ignored the legends
and Old Mary
who lives alone
at the far end
beneath the crag.

We dared
not believe, I think
in something so ancient
as we are less
by comparison
so much less
in self and time.

It shines black
a scrying mirror
to sky, sun and stars
immense distances
and awful size
threatening, dizzying
overwhelming.

Stumble by
and away
for the locals now know
not to bring their kids
or run their dogs
along that
darkly shingled shore.

Centre of the Labyrinth

it   is
not   the
fury,   heat or blood
that drives him to kill,
but the hungry madness
of the maze and defence
against those who come
with naked blades and
spears and echoing
assaults, names and
buzzing words that are
a magic he fears and
must stop
...
before it
grows violent and overtakes the moment
so he bellows and ch-a-r-g-es-s and stamps
and silence reigns once more, the closest thing to peace

Hydra

hsss   ss   ss   s   s   s
cut   here   it   leers   and   sneers
slashing   gnashing   winding binding   mesmerising
spitting acid   toxin-tipped   fangs and   scales
mul   ti   ply   ing   hid-e   ously
heads gaping maws   breath – ing   noxious
fumes to choke and blind caustically
unstringing   and   loosening
limbs and tightly held
blades and shields
sin u ous ly
finding   a way in
to end you
your crew
in a slow
agony

Wyvern

the sudden screeching   whip-winding winged
    serpent slithers   from the skies
      strikes   spikes
        with   claws
        and maw
          fangs
       shred and
       eviscerate
      . . . . .
      . . . .
        tongue
     lashes
        flames   lick
  and
  a barbed   curls
        tail   then
         brutally
  lashes   slashes
around   and
  its prey
    or foe ... they're
        all
        the same!

Cyclops

You!
who put
the I in
vanity
most cursed human incomer
selfish   sheep thief and   rude guest
breaking   the most sacred   oath
with   hosts and gods   without
care   or fear, either,   shameless Odysseus
of craven cunning
stealing   hiding
creeping   fleeing
standing no ground
name-calling as a child   so
scared of mighty Polyphemus   blinded
by night-shrouded calumny, your   dark
deed damning you ... run to your little
ship, for I smell you on the wind and these   boulders
hurled from atop this cliff shall vengefully   sink
and drown you and it will be as if you'd
never been, the waters of the sea calm
once more and hushing my roar, pain no more
than murmured
though monstrous
memories ...

Roc

Your wingspan   overarched   the sky
and eclipsed the very sun
your shadow was as cold as night
and longer than the day

You snatched up baby elephants
and fed them to your young
you dismembered human soldiers
with gaze and beak and claw

The susurrus of your feathers
was the envy of the wind
your cry defied the heavens
fearless till the end.

Mari Lywd

The bite of winter at its worst
you'll feel her approach more
than hear or see it
till the unbearable scraping
comes at your window and door
wind and weather bone-rattling and testing

the casement and seals
teasing, cajoling, pleading
in the querulous winding whispers
of air moving through the trees
coming closer
with the crackle and cackle
of fiery logs in the grate

as the moaning chimney
sounds with the lost voices
of your dearly departed
whose livid shades now visit and haunt
taunting you
for a cowering coward

who owes their living
to those gone before
the debt now to be collected
by Gray Mary
and she will lead you
from this place and world
to your overdue rest.

LOST TIMES

The Song of the Crannóg

The mud worshippers dare not attack
our mid-lake home
knowing Danu guards our refuge
is immune to fire
will drown them
will leech all heat from them
will pursue them along rivers,
out of wells, from the clouds
flush them out, wash them away
thin their food to nothing
make their blood flow too fast
and all the way out
before it can be stopped
or become to sour and bitter
that they get stomach cramps
to empty them out or are poisoned
simply, especially the young
till there aren't enough left
for the clan to continue
more than a few hands of years
at all, so that none remain
to prayer-sing their names
in their halls, at gatherings
on sacred-season days as offerings
are burnt to Dagda
will the land itself wains
and the flood waters rise
in triumph and we will swim
free and far and further
to the tops of the mountains

27

and into the skies
dousing the very sun.

Ultima Thule

Upon the windswept shores of Orkney
you'll find the Skara Brae
withstanding time and tragedy
ancient as the day

You'll recognise the stones there
though you've never been before
you'll feel the breath of ancestors
hanging in the air

You'll hear them whisper with the dawn
watching the horizon
you'll scent the storm and sailors gone
and taste the sea that rimed them

You'll wonder if you see their ghosts
as shadows grow behind you
yet do not fear this spirit host
that greets the sun anew

Far older than the pyramids
and southerly Stonehenge
their temple stands as testament
that some things do not end

Upon the windswept shores of Orkney
you'll find the Skara Brae
withstanding time and tragedy
ancient as the day.

The Broch of Gurness

We bury our dead at the threshold
to guard against wandering spirits
– they stand the long vigil of night
watching for the light

our home's aligned eastwards
to greet the rising sun
– its warmth sets us free to roam
when sleep has taken flight

the stone bones of the earth
are our fortress entire
– they keep our heat, thwart the wind
and quarrels of our enemies

giants must have been before us
to raise such a mighty hall,
a time of gods and titans
walking in our midst

in the hollows deep below
they must slumber, rest and wait
till the wheeling of the heavens
sees their glory rise again.

Vikingr

this visor
defines
your idea
of me –

the empty eye-plates
watch you

anciently

knowing

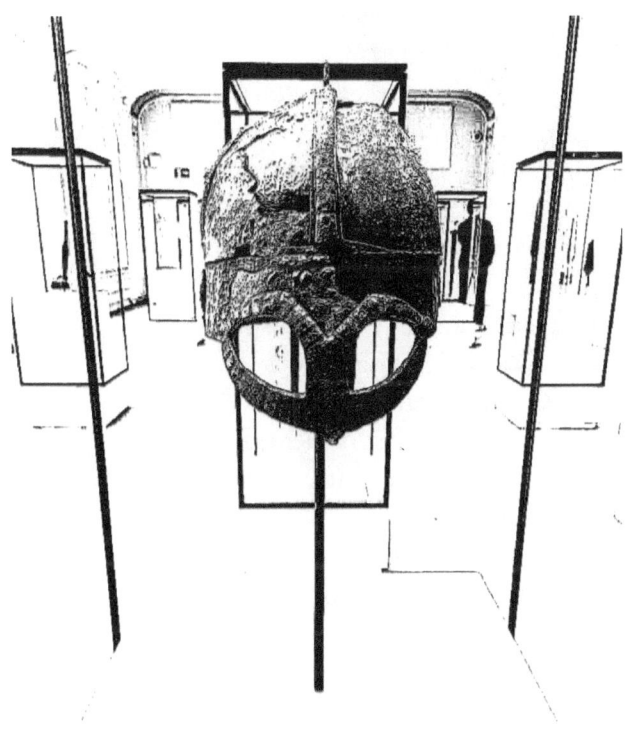

Golem

I am this lumpen thing
slow of thought
my physical body stronger
than my mind.
I am a word moulded
and animated to serve
my wizard-master
whose name I cannot form.

He had me hold back the Emperor
who aimed to execute and expel
us, and I silently drowned his soldiers
in river mud, to join the shades I'd summoned.
A girl of Prague enchanted me
for a while, yet she always fled as I followed
enraging me, and I ruined all
I could find, till the sage stilled me.

The shem was ripped from my brow
so I slept an unending sabbath
till I was called from the synagogue's store
once more, by a dark invading agent
of the new German regime
who had me stalk countless battlefields
of human ordure that none can endure
save me and my first creator.

The Maharal will find me again
as I await his instruction
direction and purpose
or another will allow me impetus …

Via ritual, transport or curse
– I cannot fathom differently
though I ponder who in turn
so powers mortals and their wants.

Could that other then not speak to me
and frame me all anew
to offer me more appetite
to be and even do?
Till then I watch them passing by
an ignored, unmoving statue
it's me who lasts too long, I think
– they're far too quick for me.

Banshee

Why cannot omens be undone!
They visit ill thoughts and fears
upon us, adding punishment
to what is to come
praps even depressing all
to bring about that promised doom.

There, beneath the low trees
crouched the dark fairy-wife
lamenting our cursed house
her song heard across the woods
warning well-wishers away
and calling the dark coach onwards.

A headless spectre drives the horses
come to fetch a soul
he will not leave without one
yet I cannot give up my kin
I dare not
for I am nothing without them.

Yet the siren is strangely soft now
enchanting, a murmur of memories
as if stories spoken at a wake
fondly bidding farewell to the phantom
of fellow, family and folly
ah, then, I see it is me that they await.

LOST WORLDS

radon daughter

It was Rutherford in 1899
who claimed her as his own
her existence and half-life
confined to a basement
an unsafe emanation
otherwise not there.

Unstable, he called her
rarer than any other
but dangerous, to be guarded
against, like an exhaled curse
or barely luminescent ghost
a haunting Typhoid Mary.

And so he trapped her there
by permafreezing time
– like an insect in amber –
a trophy to his boast
of her radioactive power
made visible, on display.

Yet the sciences of man
– ambition, war and grief –
cracked the very Earth
in a seismic release:
and in the hair-trigger cascade
she finally slipped away.

The Archaeology of Yarn

... strange skeletons
of dwelling places perhaps
peek up through the sands
like hidden leviathans
or predators crouched in ambush
... we dare not come closer
to these psychic graves
for an old madness lingers there
and no good can come of it
though their ancient pain still calls
... we avoid the stone-carved footprints
that lead towards the awful depths
and vast chambers
of their necropolis
where they restlessly demand new worship
... insatiable were their lives
until all was simply exhausted
maybe we do follow them
in some ways then
and their kind is come again ...

The Iridescent Seas of Yarn

… sand comes blowing in waves
… rainbows dancing in cosmic rays
life causes not even a ripple …
long since buried beneath ancient dunes …
… radiation spirals and gyres
… kaleidoscopically
a blinding and pretty eye-blight …
a tsunami and awful delight …
… I don't know why I came here
… my expectancy can't be high
there's naught but riddling runes …
and moons like coloured balloons …
… quick obscured by tumults of dust
… and rivulets of wasted tears
why do I record this message …
a eulogy to this barren refuge …
… final words to mark my passing
… remember me if you find them …

The Ghosts of Yarn

The broken landscape refracts beautifully
bloody reds in the dark maw of the sky
as if eaten alive, drooling rainbows
stringing out, stretched and thin.

Some vestige remains, they all swear
though scanners – malfunctioning – report only absence:
visitors to this death-planet speak
of a swirl of starring hues that distract
and mesmerise, mazing thoughts creating
a mind-labyrinth where a restless legacy lurks.

Many fail to return, blindly lost
the few witnesses whispering of wayward
visions of vast hulks hunkering low
waiting for the wheel of space to turn.

It's said the ancient empire seeded
and festooned the cosmos
enslaving whole galaxies for millennia
yet all became exhausted somehow
collapsing and crashing and scattering
irradiated to dust and carried off on solar winds.

There are raving claims of hidden pools
of sentient water that'll flood the senses
and gut you as surely as any weapon
then to spit you out.

And maddened musings that the air is parasitic
using you for mere gas-exchange

then leaving you empty
gasping like a fish
or a punctured lung
wetly wheezing its last.

There's no safe ground, it'll eat your feet
entangle you, subside under you
lead you to deadfalls like throats
turning you to mulch and manure.

Some vestige remains, waiting
visitors speak, restless
witnesses whisper low, exhausted
collapsing and raving claims
spit out, empty and punctured –
haunted by endless echoes.

An Intergalactic Interlude

The iridescent seas of Yarn
Still fizz with radiation,
The tourist-ships that brought us here
Perhaps an explanation.
The mutants thrashing deep below
All fight intoxication
And try to charm us to our deaths
With siren ululation.
Their plaintiff wailing haunts me now
In thoughts and swelling dreams
They're mermaid-quick and rainbow-ripe,
Or that is how it seems.
The eye of one, it found me out
And in this darkness gleams
It stares and stares as if to warn –
I know not what it means.
They say that Yarn was once pristine,
Jewel of the cosmic crown,
That all that dwelt upon its face
Then learned to swim or drown.
The rise of civilizations
Thus will see us all come down
For Entropy, unwelcome guest
Looks on us with a frown

Penal Colony 045

Steve came down with the Sickness
so he suffered isolation
– slow and sudden
the sadness of his spiral
twisted and wanting
and wasting away.

The mines are crowded and close
the air skeleton thin and starving
the radiation cooks you down to the marrow
till your eyeballs fizz
in their sockets and your mind
leaks from your ears.

The stars twinkle and blink
disbelievingly
to see us spinning
through the void
on our prison moon
to nowhere.

The transport offloaded today
exchanging new exiles
for precious expandium
to power the Empire's fleet
ambition and exploration
for new glories and heavens.

I've lost track now
of time, conversations
debts and favours, my term

of sentence, even my original offence
one of my few remaining memories that
this is all we deserve.

The sweet escape of mind-sleep
while the body works autonomically
means I hardly know I'm here
– it's a blessing really
and makes existence bearable
my ghost-self entirely wearable.

NEW REALITIES

t
h **Superstring**
r
e
I guess   a
there was a loose d   somewhere and someone decided to pull it
cos everything began to unravel … it's not easy to knit it back as
we don't have the needles small enough – yet we'll have to patch
it somehow even it isn't an invisible mend and makes everything
look rough and ready, and any holidaying alien might be severely
unimpressed and leave a bad Space Tripadvisor review, and then
our galactic stock will really plummet and the neighbours will say
we're lowering the tone of the area, and then the Inspectors will turn
up and level some sort of fine if we even get off that easy and aren't
delisted or, worse, entirely condemned, perhaps to be scrapped so
they can go with a complete new build, without idiot humans – see
what happens when you pull

a loose thread?

Chronovirus

so it transpires
Time was a virus all along
and we catch it as babes
through mother's milk,
contact
with every hyperinfected surface
even the air though
we haven't identified any
particulate nature as yet
– Oxford are working on a cure
but fear we're too late, like
chasing that watch-clutching
quick and mazing white rabbit
as it escapes the lab before
we can isolate the pathogen
mesmerised by tiktok hands,
whirling and eye-twisting,
dizzyingly till we queasily drop-stop
– from space it came, they
speculate, an alien life-form
or attack, praps
a contagion-message not to venture
beyond our environs
and limiting nature
since we're not welcome
with our weaknesses
amongst the immortals.

A Public Safety Announcement

The strange thoughts you've been having
aren't your own naturally
nor the denial, disbelief and forgetting

don't trust yourself to keep reading
these words of warning now your awareness
has alerted that which possesses you

instead increase your mindfulness
and retrospectively monitor
all you said and did before

repeating it over and over
so they can't keep it all erased,
and make notes for yourself

that you'll find so you'll be reminded
of who you once were and might be
again given some sort of cure

yet we don't know how to stop them
how they arrived and came to infect us
whether they're old but newly released demons

a curse, a virus or parasite
whose goal is to undo us all
– don't listen to those who say otherwise

for we've connected such fervent individuals
to the sudden rise in terrorist acts
against institutions, states and the world

And please, please, please, if you can
don't hesitate to spread the word
– they're here and you might be one of them.

The Surgeon

He mastered a cut so fine
it was invisible –
nothing came apart until
so much
later that cause
and effect were in bits
and pieces
for the
police and even then
putting it all together again
so that it began to make sense
was a gory jigsaw puzzle
– except it wasn't
because the blood didn't go back in
nor the hairs, nails and intestines
and the flesh wouldn't go back
on the bones
– yet DNA
was the real shock
because the sequences had
been s e p a r a t e d, the spirals
unravelled and left lying like
limp spaghetti, unstrung
so there was no way of knowing
who they'd been
if they'd even existed
whether we could leave anything
of meaning when our time came
and existentially we understood
the great unmaker.

A J Dalton

The Simulation

coming home
after the accident
there's something wrong

all appears normal
or, rather, too precisely that
so not the same

the colours are off
sounds are tinny
often from too far away

the betraying sign:
I love you, she tells me
and Julia has never said that!

who is this person
living with me
I'm suddenly scared

they warned me
it might feel like this
but, then, they would say that

to cover up
for how they've replaced everything
to keep me trapped

in a virtual world
or managed environment
though I did nothing wrong

but there's no one
I can tell
cos they're stooges

smiling informants,
warders, who don't want me
to know I'm in a prison

Technorati

... in the beginning was the word on the street
they were no longer human
reprogrammed by their machines
or mentally cross-integrated
certainly, the word fertilised was an abomination
as the technoprophets of the digital church said
in every binary tongue
in Klingon and speculated languages
in the cryptic multivalent systems
and codes with only their own names
I saw the best minds of my own generation
dragged hither and thither down virtual streets
arrested with Ginsberg, thrown into the back
of simulated wagons and hauled off
to the electric wilderness
to run free as naked screaming loons
– better than in a voyeuristic prison or zoo, eh?
repopulating the human wastelands with a breeding stock
and keeping them safely out of the cyber centres
restoring them to what they once were
and should be again.
Praps they aren't neon overlords or shining saviours: instead
thought riddling oracles and hieroglyphic propagandists
gaslighting us with burning helium, toxins and fixes
my father gasped as he closed his eyes
to rest with the smile of angels
upon his dear dear face.
I try to lift my head like Atlas
but only shift that precariously precious weight
of my world carried between my shoulders:

he refused the Final Upload
and I cannot understand.

NEW REALMS

Gulliver's Travels to the Farthest Reaches

1 The Land of the Technopomps

He swam as fortune directed
And foundered on a shore
Where exhaustion quickly claimed him
How long he did not know
Yet awake he did at last
To find himself constrained
By wheel-cogs, levers & struts:
Where the more he struggled,
The more he powered a surrounding mechanism,
An interlocking world of darkly moving parts
Then as he realised he was its battery caged
And slowed in stark dismay
His captors came to peer at him
In beady-eyed affront.
"This discipline will civilize you
And improve your efficiency,
The better to drive the working whole.
Thus, man-thing, please set to!"
He strained with shaking limbs
And unfed failing strength
Ceasing as he begged that they understand his rights.
"You've contributed nothing and earned about the same;
The Technopomps command you
To push on out of shame."
He cried he did not know them
Nor recognise their kind,
Their beeping tones and brittle bits
Nor that ticking, grinding shift.

They mocked his brutish moaning
And praised their Technorati
Whose existence went to maintain
The Supreme Technician's design.
But he came to see they were small –
Only large through trick of a lens –
He summoned the last that he had
And broke free of the ordering housing.
He fled their shrieking alarms
Down shining mirrored paths
And came to a controlling tower
Which took off once he entered.

2 The Land of the Hedons

The thrust crushed him flat and he fainted
Seeing skies, stars and moons in his mind
Till he landed on a planet
Paradise of poppies, sporting youths and colour.
They welcomed him like a child
Their disarming physiques on display
"Come with us," they murmured, "to learn and share in our ways,
Be naturalised
And strip your habits bare."
They pulled him on and teased
At his clothing and he bid them stay
Though their strength was much
To prevent all rebuff.
"Our customs and habits are holy
We Hedons rejoice in the body
As the gift of the Spirit of Life

So unguard yourself now, wee stranger!"
He pleaded he did not know them
Nor understand their needs;
They promised still to use him
As their desire and will intended.
Therefore he feared them too large
In appetite and endless demand,
And hurried till utterly spent
To their Well of Infinite Depth.

3 The Land of Realists and Positivists

In he went despite their pleas
Tumbling head over heels for an age
Or more until he splashed down
In a lake of cushioned weeds.
He breathed relief and made a land
All well-maintained and brimming
Albeit half was solid and red
The other all bluish and whimsy.
Their factions came and begged his vote
Their numbers exactly even,
He scratched his head and asked their case,
Their arguments to be made.
"The blues are useless dreamers
All caught up in impossible futures
While Realists are properly grounded
Dealing with the here and now."
"No! The reds are utterly selfish
Caring only for immediate interests
Where we Positivists project and plan

To change all things entire."
He saw them equally earnest
passionate and intent
And finally gave his judgement
They would have to live apart.
They recoiled in outraged horror
Spouses, partners and children crying
Refusing to split their families
And turning upon the monster!

4 The Land of the Speaking Beasts

They chased him to the border
And he became a refugee
In a place of imagination
Where animals spoke and ruled:
They put him in a zoo
Since they knew his sort of old
And trusted him not at all
Though fascinating he was.
His home was well provisioned
With morsels and creature comforts
For a while he was quite content
As he recovered all he'd been.
Till viewer-visitors came to taunt him
And his kindly sheep-headed keepers
Insisted he exercise more
– He only felt ashamed
For once having eaten such souls.
As much as he wanted to remain
They thought less of him day by day

So at last by mutual consent
They went their separate ways.

5 The Land of His Britannic Majestie
Having carved out a long canoe
He paddled by the sun and stars
Into familiar waters:
Where a friendly Portuguese ferried him
To Albion at last!
His wondrous tales enthralled them
And inclined their sweet ambition
Yet strongly did he warn them
That nothing might be gained:
"Such lands are best avoided
In respect of essential difference
We should build defence and alliance
For when they come to us."

Spirit Sleuth

blink rapidly, stare
fixedly, relax your gaze
you'll see them

their shadows clustered
clinging to the ceiling
waiting for you to sleep

you'll struggle
to wake, dream-fuddled
exhausted and drained

you can't blame them
for not wanting to fade
out of existence entirely

yet they're not
your ghosts of lives
cruelly taken:

there must be a murderer
in the area dispossessing
bodies of their spirits

maybe a mumbling medium
can channel
something useful, for once

or better to do it yourself
door-to-door to explore
awkward absences and lonely silences

to discover clues or a pattern
as to what's happened
and what won't anymore

usually it's someone unblinking
but there are whispers of late
of a something

insatiable and inescapable
ancient and inexplicable
so I fear that I will find it

alone, alert or waiting
for me, as I'm tiring
and fully unexceptional

though there's a new priest in town
so young and fresh and sweet
succulent, some might say

an encumbrance probably
or an unholy coincidence
to arrive at such a time

but I'm out of friends and options
and maybe he's a sign:
God has sent me some help

at long bloody last.

Cloud People

the ground disappears
beneath their feet
as fast as they can build
columns   towers   and battlements:
castles in the air warring widely against
winds and fortune, each other
all in slow motion
until
strikes   bolts   gales
devastate and tumble walls
photo-stricken giants railing
and howling for the loss
of their heavenly estate
angels thwarting their tempestuous ascent
sweeping and clearing all away
with the coming of the day

below, the rolling earth grinds its daily round
ponderous with graves and gravitas, golems of lumpen clay
heavy-headed, bowed and weighted, dreaming of the sky

On a Wing and a Prayer

flung into the heavens
on our little rocket ship
we don't know where we're going
we've made a mess of it

we'll find a world to live on
or else we simply won't
some think we shouldn't bother
and others, well, they don't

it's about our civilization
and its over-riding value
alright we caused destruction
but we'll learn from it anew

we'll avoid our previous errors
we'd be stupid otherwise
and should it all disintegrate
we'll deserve our quick demise

Darker Darkest

in the deep shadows
of the furthest space
where light never returns

there lurks
the unseen
end-being and end-time

envisioned only
by blind seers
unhinged prophets

the apocalyptically insane
witchkind
and god-cursed poets

Nether Realm

Do not ask of that place
for knowledge then will haunt you.

Guard yourself against whisperings
as they'll serve only to mislead you

down dark alleys, twisting turns
all roundabout up and down

till you're lost at last and
you reach your dead end.

NEW DARKNESSES

Denizens

of the nether realm
they

wait

for ever
and for you

their patience eternal

like the dark mountains
of doom and forgetting.

The Ritual

He will conduct you
– the dark servant –
into the sanctum
maleficarum

tomes of ages:
still and silent witnesses
to the bloody sacrifices

since the dawn
of the immense reign
and conjuration upon Earth
of Narzule.

The Dark Magician

At last he walked the Nether Realm
searching
for his love
lost ages past

and found her
captive to the rule most cruel
of the fell god
Narzule

who demanded a terrible price
for a resurrection
of her life
and short it would be:

yet the mage agreed
the terms
beyond caring
for himself

his grief-addled mind
its own prison
punishment
and torture

so she was returned
into his arms again
confused, alarmed and haunted
not her former self;

she would not hear his pleas
about how they used to be
too troubled and tormented
by all that she had seen –

he understood his error then
death could not be undone
save as a living lie
and that had cost his soul.

Man Grove

In the dark magician's garden
bodies slowly writhe, pinned by wooden stakes:
growing from their chests
bloody blooms of flowering mandrakes.

In the dark magician's garden
there's moaning and grrrroooaning
whimpering and pleas
for mercy and death.

In the dark magician's garden
roots ease into arteries
releasing a paralysing toxin
to prevent too much tormented struggle.

In the dark magician's garden
the miasma of human manure and mulch
is thick and busy with flies
around nose and mouth and eyes.

Perhaps you'll visit my garden one day
and enjoy the hungry flora
I'll cannibalise a salad for us
and we'll catch up on old times.

Phantasm

In the shattered light of morning
colours separate and clash, warring
ghastly reds splashing blood
painting a scene to appal
me, my nerves, and immolate
my thoughts and memory
of what happened, conjuring it
afresh, her hands reaching for me
to visit the same mercy
she'd begged of me, my own beloved
so weak at the awful end
but now a vengeful apparition
to haunt my conscience
and mind, my days and life whole
an existence which is torture
more than anything else,
a purgatory of harrowing grief
where we cannot be together
as we once were, victims
of ourselves and our former happiness,
both of us livid wraiths
railing against the doom of love
and loss and humanity,
the cruel mockery of birdsong
heralding the rising sun
which had shone on us abed once
when we held each other in the dawn
of our marriage, those blessed moments
of youth which are as a new curse
to this ageing individual –
Ah! Would that we could both find rest finally.

Ecohorror II

He came for me
To end me
Weapon naked
To slice my throat open
And disembowel me
This noble warrior
Of the Church of Civilization:
Hard-eyed
Iron-clad
Scripture-fed –
He found me out
Like those before him
In the darkest depths
Of my fern-feathered refuge
Where I'd hidden from the hateful world
And the martial followers of the He-god
Yet the sky had gathered
The forest had stilled
And the air had tasted of metal –
As the predator came stalking closer:
So I knew of his approach
Terror silently choking me
I conjured my animal-spirit tattoos
To beset the relentless soldier
Simply, he shrugged them off like shadows
No seeming care for the familiars sacrificed
Now he had me cornered
Eyes, teeth and blade aglitter
In a desperate prayer to the goddess, though
I channelled through ley lines for lodestones
That slowed him, all the while

79

Raising ground water upwards to have his armour bring him low
How mightily he fought the nature that made him
Even … I made him a companionable offer –
Alas, he would have nothing of mercy
So there he drowned spitting 'Witch!'
With that his final breath
And all just because, to ensure my continued youthfulness
I'd consumed a few of their infants
Such a shame, such a shame.

NEW DREAMS

The Starry Night

... a nanomite
on a quantum flight
or a darkling quark
on a sacred arc
into the skies
where grounding dies
yet no one mourns
as dreams are born ...

After Marianne Stokes

the maiden
rose up
in her bed
to find the grey messenger
awaiting

her silent appeal:
fear-filled
timid and terrible
for her children
as yet unborn;

the pitying stillness
the only answer
shadowy wings overarching
a poise as remorseless
as forever

Technocracy

They know what I want
before I do, in fact
I have no wants
save want of a want
strange feeling that
for which I'm medicated rightly
distracted monitored refracted
for my own good
lest I disrupt corrupt interrupt
the wider social programme
be too abrupt or erupt
for our own good
or risk being unplugged disconnected
alone
horrendously endlessly messily lessly
worse than dying or not being uploaded
my series terminated and erased
without back-up or restoration point
and all because of want of a want
wantonly wan tons in tonnes
yes, sorry silly – it's just so
that I can't
stop

Technosavant

Cyber zen is the state
of mind, of affairs and of play
they say
but I wouldn't know
my interface failed young
so I'm stateless, unintegrated, disintegrated
technically disabled
I had a friend: Sheila 243
as pretty as can be
we'd play and daydream
in pixel fields and wireless wishlists
about desire-dragons and divinity games
yet she ascended on digi-wings
and I'm left down here
to daydream
of Sheila 243 pretty as can be
when she was my friend
with me, playing
I wonder if it was the mesh device
or me that was wrong,
whether I can cut my brain
into the right shape
it has to be
worth a try
right?
To see her again.
Would it change me?
Would she remember me?
so pretty as can be

Technomancer

The mind-wizards murmur
and thought-witches tattle and cackle
– their static crackles!
I try to keep myself
from them
But they have my signature now
I'm hunted
through the cyberlands
down digi-gorges, up virtual mountains
across electric planes, into neon-dark
of tattooed transport, instant issue
nerve-stretched nirvanas and neverworlds.
Yet I scrabble together ingredients –
toe of new route, and eye of electrode
into my encrypted cauldron
for one great broadcasting
of a conjured spell-familiar
to sniff-detect them out
of their reality-remote lairs
into the spell-bright highlight sun
and then
Then!
Hahahaha.

Designing Daisies

getting the white just right
will drive you mad
but it's worth it

to see them nodding at you
in a gentle breeze
nature steadily restored

now that we've realised it isn't
about us actually

– and that shade of yellow in the centre
richer than the sun
or an egg yolk

offset by the pale petals
you've so painstakingly worked on
for what feels like forever

will reward you like freshly churned butter
melting into crumpets

– and techno-bees will buzz busily
as they delightedly detect
nectar

and pollinate
the wide world wildly
creating anew

mornings dewy jewelled
and rainbow-refracted
for me and you.

Acknowledgements

I am hugely grateful to British artist Bruce Pennington (www.brucepennington.co.uk) for permitting us to use *The Barley Tower* as the cover art for this collection. The Green Man (aka Herne the Hunter) sat atop the tower is a perfect evocation. In his time, Bruce has, of course, been cover artist for the holy trinity of Arthur C. Clarke, Isaac Asimov and Robert Heinlein, not to mention Frank Herbert!

I am just as hugely grateful to Justin Sloane of Starship Sloane Publishing (of which Wild Man of the Woods Press is an imprint). Justin's unfailing efforts, good faith and effervescent enthusiasm are a rare tonic indeed, to keep you going through the dark months ... along with a dram of whisky.

Before this collection was compiled, the following poems were individually published in (or accepted for publication by) the following magazines and journals:

'Hunting Herne', *Quadrant*, 2026.

'Jupiter', *Empyrean* 15, Sept 2025.

'Centre of the Labyrinth', *The Mythic Circle* 48, 2026.

'Ultima Thule', *The Mythic Circle* 47, July 2025.

'Golem', *Dreams and Nightmares* 131, Oct 2025.

'The Archaeology of Yarn', *Penumbric Speculative Fiction Magazine*, 2026.

'An Intergalactic Interlude', *BFS Horizons* 18, 2026.

'Superstring', *Trollbreath* 6, Dec 2025.

'Chronovirus', *Star*Line* 48.2, April 2025.

'A Public Safety Announcement', *Mobius: The Journal of Social Change* 36:2, May 2025.

'The Surgeon', *JOURN-E* 4:1, May 2025.

'Technorati', *Star*Line* 47.3, July 2024.

'Gulliver's Travels to the Farthest Reaches', *Sublimation* 2:2, May 2025.

'Spirit Sleuth', *Spectral Realms* 24, Jan 2026.

'Darker Darkest', *Star*Line* 48.3, July 2025.

'The Dark Magician', *Eldritch Prayers*, ed. Ted Sunhede Fulk (Island of Wak-Wak, Oct 2025).

'Man Grove', *Horrorzine*, March 2025.

'Phantasm', *New Isles Press* 4, March 2025.

'Technomancer', *Gothic Nature Journal* 5, May 2025.

About the Author

A J DALTON (www.ajdalton.eu) lives in Shepherd's Bush, London, with his monstrous cat, Cleopatra. He (Adam, not the cat) is a prize-winning author of fantasy, science fiction and horror. He has published the *Empire of the Saviours* trilogy with Gollancz, *The Book of the Witches* and other collections with Kristell Ink, and *The Satanic in Science Fiction and Fantasy* with Luna Press Publishing.

Green Man Ascendant is his second poetry collection; his first collection, titled *Dark Woods Rising*, is also published by Wild Man of the Woods Press. He did his best, and his mum's proud.